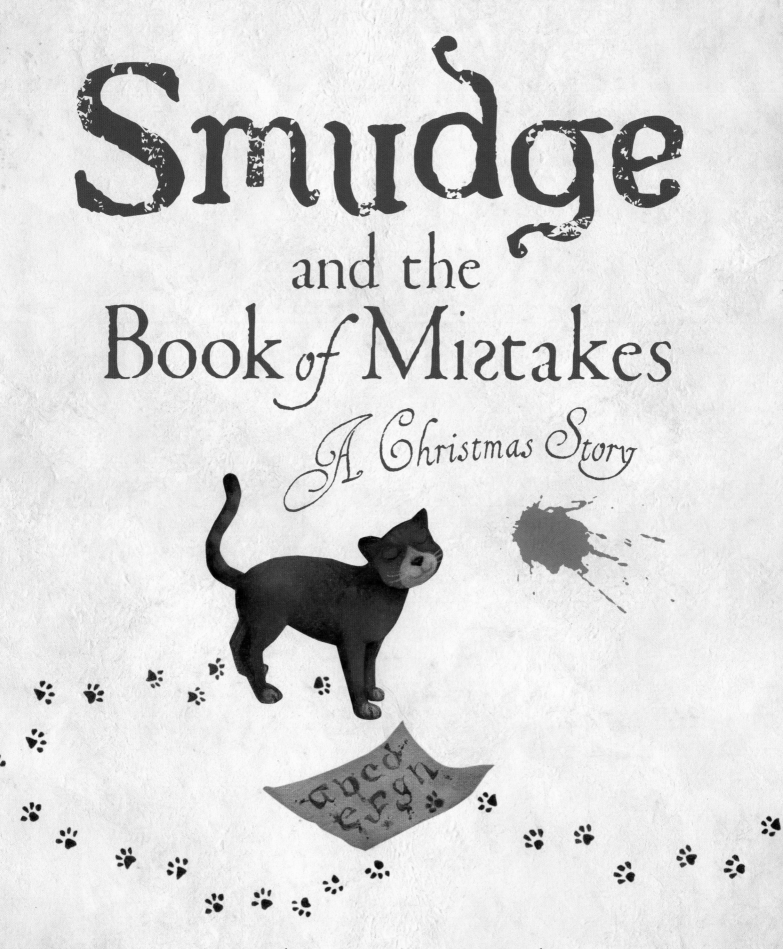

Smudge

and the
Book of Mistakes

A Christmas Story

Written by Gloria Whelan & Illustrated by Stephen Costanza

The cruel winter winds blew across Ireland and over the sea to the island of Morcarrick, frosting the stone walls of the monastery of St. Ambrose and turning the water in the monks' washbasins to ice. Cuthbert sat shivering in his cell, reflecting on his failures.

Cuthbert had been sent to the monastery after his father saw the boy would be hopeless as a warrior. Cuthbert was not big, but small and pale like a seedling that has just emerged from the ground.

He was an impatient boy who gave up easily. When crumbled under the weight of heavy metal armor, he would not put the armor on again. He refused to retrieve his sword of iron after it slipped from his weak grasp. He gave up archery on his first try because the arrows missed their target. When he was thrown from his horse, he refused to climb back on.

Cuthbert said, "If I try a thing once and I fail, why would I try it again?"

Outraged, Cuthbert's father cried, "Send him to the monks!"

Cuthbert was fifteen when he arrived at the monastery of St. Ambrose. The sleeves of his robe swallowed his hands; his hood fell over his face, blinding him, so that he was forever bumping into things.

He found the monks' behavior strange. When they were disobedient or said something unkind, they didn't wait to be punished. They hurried to punish themselves. They went without their meal; fasting, they called it. When Cuthbert did something *he* was ashamed of he liked to comfort himself by eating an extra bit of bread and honey to make *himself* feel better.

And there was the choir. Like the cicadas that sing in the trees, the monks chanted all day long and in the night as well. The sound of their plainsong was sweet, but when Cuthbert opened his mouth, his voice sounded like the crows that perch on the monastery roof.

"You must practice," the choirmaster said.

"If you do something badly," Cuthbert said, "why do it over and over?"

The monks tried him in the kitchen but he refused to learn how to gather honey after a bee stung him. He was assigned to the sewing room but he would not practice his stitching and the robe he made for Brother John fell apart, exposing Brother John's underwear.

Thinking he could do little harm with a goose quill, they put Cuthbert into the scriptorium where the lettering was done. Cuthbert was happy in the scriptorium. He liked letters. Each letter had its own unique story to tell. The **H** with the two little rooms, one on top of the other. The ups and downs of the **M** and **W**. The **X**, like crossed swords. And he had a wonderful idea for **X**. Why could you not put a little tail on the end of one of the swords?

He suggested the little tail to Brother Bede, who was in charge of the scriptorium. Brother Bede laughed and laughed. Then he gave Cuthbert a slap and told him to hold his tongue.

In Cuthbert's eagerness to make the letters he so loved, he dribbled and blotted the ink. His pages looked like a flock of blackbirds had settled on them. Brother Ethbert, who was the best scribe in the monastery and knew it, took to calling Cuthbert "Smudge." It was time to shift Cuthbert to another job.

On the Feast of Saint Blaise the very ancient and stubborn Abbot of St. Ambrose called for Brother Bede. Brother Bede bowed a very low bow. He trembled, for it was known that the abbot was strict and would not put up with so much as a whisker of disagreement.

"It is very cold today, Abbot," Brother Bede said.

"What do you mean I look very old today!" the hard-of-hearing abbot said. "Why wouldn't I with fools like you to deal with?"

When Brother Bede tried to explain what he had said, the abbot raised his hand for silence. "I have something of the greatest importance to say to you. I have chosen our own Brother Gregory, the finest illuminator of manuscripts in the world, to illustrate the Christmas Story. The manuscript will be praised throughout the world."

The abbot smiled. "And, of course, so will the abbot and monastery from whence it came. I must have your very best scribe to provide the lettering."

"There can be no question," Brother Bede said. "Brother Ethbert is the one. He never makes a mistake."

"Then go at once to the scriptorium and tell Cuthbert I wish to see him."

"I'm afraid you misunderstood, dear Father Abbot. Not Cuthbert, Brother *Ethbert*."

"What! You said Cuthbert. Why are you arguing with me? I won't have disagreement. Now, off with you."

Brother Bede scurried back to the scriptorium. Wringing his hands he told his story to Brother Ethbert.

Brother Ethbert hopped from one foot to the other. His face reddened. His eyes narrowed. His words came out with a lot of spit. "Impossible! A catastrophe! Didn't you tell Father Abbot that I am the greatest scribe in Ireland, if not the world? Didn't you tell the abbot he made a mistake?"

"Tell the abbot he was mistaken?"

"No, I suppose you could not do that, but the thought of Smudge is ridiculous. We must go to Brother Gregory and explain what has happened. When he hears about Smudge he'll hurry to the abbot himself. The abbot thinks so well of Brother Gregory's work he is sure to listen to him."

Brother Gregory sat alone in his cell. On his worktable were pots of paint. There were brushes, some so fine they had only a hair or two. There was a mortar and pestle to grind the colors. Lying on the table were sheets of parchment. Brother Gregory had all he needed to begin what would surely be the greatest achievement of his career: illustrating the Christmas Story. He loved St. Luke's words and knew them all by heart.

But he asked of himself, "How can I create this great work if Brother Ethbert is to be the scribe?" He was sure Brother Ethbert would be chosen, for everyone in the monastery said he was the best scribe. All his letters marched in neat rows. But Brother Ethbert's letters had no heart to them, no imagination. Brother Ethbert did not love his letters.

What was worse, Brother Ethbert was bossy and would tell him what to do. He would quarrel with everything Brother Gregory attempted so that Brother Gregory would lose heart. If he lost heart his work would still get done, but it would not be a great work.

Just then Brother Ethbert and Brother Bede crowded into Brother Gregory's cell, both of them talking at once. They related their story and Brother Ethbert urged, "You must go at once to see the abbot and tell him a dreadful mistake has been made."

When Brother Gregory learned he might not have to work with Brother Ethbert, he gave silent thanks to the Blessed Virgin.

He told the two monks, "Surely you can see I could never tell the abbot he has made a mistake. It's unthinkable. You know how stubborn he is."

"But you don't understand," Brother Bede said. "He has confused Brother Ethbert with Smudge."

"Smudge?"

"Well, that's what we call Cuthbert because he is forever ruining perfectly good parchment with his blots."

Blots! Brother Gregory winced. He looked at the pure white parchment that lay on the table. He was about to hurry to the abbot when Brother Ethbert said in the bossy voice Brother Gregory hated, "I am anxious to tell you all *my* ideas for your illustrations."

Brother Gregory took a deep breath. "I'm very sorry but I couldn't possibly contradict the abbot. I'll just have to make the best of the abbot's mistake. And after the abbot has seen Smudge, send him to me."

The abbot gazed upon the bundle of wool Smudge made as he bowed. "Get up off the floor, Cuthbert. One can carry submission too far." Though in his heart of hearts the abbot did not see how. "I understand you are the monastery's finest scribe. An amazing accomplishment for one so young."

Smudge, overwhelmed at being in the presence of the abbot, found his words all glued together so that he could not separate one from the other.

The abbot was not unhappy to see how properly awed the young man was in his presence. "Now, now, speak up."

"Oh, dear Abbot, please don't mock me. I know very well my lettering is messy and scrawly."

"Modesty is fine up to a point. I suppose Brother Bede has told you that you have been chosen to work with Brother Gregory?"

"No, indeed. He didn't say a word to me. I would be so honored to assist Brother Gregory." Smudge saw himself scrubbing Brother Gregory's floors and dusting his manuscripts.

"No daydreaming!" the abbot interrupted Smudge's thoughts. "Now off you go to Brother Gregory."

Brother Gregory noticed Smudge standing at his doorway. "What do you want?" he asked. "I can't be disturbed now, I'm expecting someone."

"The abbot sent me. I'm Smudge, the scribe. I'm very sorry."

"What are you sorry about? And why are you shaking?"

"I'm shivering."

"Come in, come in. Put down your hood and let me see your face. Why, you are just a youth! Warm your hands by the fire and then show me a sample of your script."

Smudge felt the warmth of the room comfort him like a mother's arms. Oh, to spend his days in this room … but why was Brother Gregory asking to see a sample of his script when all he would be doing would be keeping Brother Gregory's cell tidy? Smudge knew he would be sent away the moment Brother Gregory saw his rude and shapeless scribbles. Who would want so careless a creature cleaning his precious brushes and paints?

To gain a few moments in the warm room, Smudge said, "I'm afraid my hands have gone all numb from the cold."

"Hold them near the fire and while they are thawing you can tell me something of your approach to letters."

Here was something Smudge could talk about. "I'm very fond of letters, Brother Gregory. I love the way each letter has its own little story to tell. The **H** with the two little rooms just alike. The ups and downs of the **M** and **W**. The **X**, like crossed swords."

Brother Gregory was delighted. Here was a monk who thought for himself. He would be a pleasure and an inspiration to work with. Who would have believed someone so young would be so clever?

But there was something else that had to be asked. "Do you have any ideas about my illuminations?"

"Ideas for *you*? Oh my, I know nothing about illuminating a story. You are the very best in Ireland. How could I presume to give *you* ideas?"

Brother Gregory smiled with satisfaction. "Your fingers should be thawed out. Let me see a sample of your lettering."

"I am only going to tidy your room, Brother Gregory. Why would you wish to see my lettering?"

"Tidy my room? What are you talking about? You are going to provide the lettering for the Christmas Story."

He handed Smudge a goose quill, some ink, and a small sheet of parchment which Brother Gregory kept just for practice.

Smudge took the quill with trembling hands. He dipped it in the black ink. He made his favorite letter, **H**. The sides were wriggly. The middle sloped. There was a blot of ink as large as a raisin.

Brother Gregory covered his eyes with his hands to shut out the horror. Hopeless. He would have to go to the abbot and tell him he must have Brother Ethbert. Then what? Neat but boring lettering. Brother Ethbert's endless interference with his painting.

Yet here was this boy who loved letters. Who thought about them all the time. He would mind his own business. Given time and practice might he learn to be a scribe?

Brother Gregory said, "Smudge, you are to be here tomorrow morning the second the cock crows. Now leave me. I must see the abbot."

The moment he was alone Brother Gregory dipped a brush in carmine paint and then in white to make a bright pink. Carefully, for he did everything carefully, he painted his right hand with the pink paint and let it dry.

"Dear Abbot," Brother Gregory said, "I'm afraid I have bad news."

The abbot frowned. Given a choice between good news and bad news he preferred good news.

"In shifting the wood for my fire I burned my right hand." Counting on the abbot's ancient eyesight he held out his hand with its painted pink skin. "With God's grace my hand will heal and be good as new."

"But the Christmas Story! What of the Christmas Story?"

"Father Abbot, you know that before something truly beautiful can be created there must be a great many musings, a great many ponderings of ideas. Before you give us those thoughtful sermons that reassure and calm us each Sunday, you must spend many hours in meditation."

The abbot liked the sound of the words "reassure" and "calm." On Sunday after Sunday he looked out with distress at the monks' nodding heads. Now he was being told his sermons calmed them. And what does one do when one is calmed? One closes one's eyes and rests. He felt better.

"By all means, take as much time as you need."

"Thank you for being so kind."

"Of course, I don't mind. Now go along to your cell."

As Brother Gregory passed the scriptorium, Brother Bede popped out.

"Were you talking with the abbot? Complaining about Smudge? Insisting on Brother Ethbert?"

"Not at all. I'm more than pleased with Smudge."

"You're not serious? The fool can't draw a single letter without a mistake."

"Of course, there must be a little practice but the abbot has kindly given me extra time."

Brother Bede was almost speechless but not quite. "Then you actually mean to use Smudge?"

"Yes, indeed."

Brother Bede scurried to confer with Brother Ethbert.

Brother Ethbert said, "He is a very impatient boy. He will never practice his letters."

"No stick-to-it-tive-ness at all," Brother Bede agreed. "It is only a matter of days before Brother Gregory changes his mind."

The following morning Smudge appeared in Brother Gregory's cell. He had a scrub brush in one hand and a pail in the other for nothing could make him believe he was to print the words for the Christmas Story.

"Enough of this foolishness," Brother Gregory said, "put away the pail. You are about to become the finest scribe in Ireland."

"But you have seen my work. It's rough and messy."

"It's ideas that count and you have excellent ideas. You will make a fine scribe. You have only to practice."

"Practice? You mean do something over and over? If you try something once and it doesn't work, why would you be foolish enough to keep trying it?"

"Smudge, I'm going to show you something that I have never shown another living soul."

Brother Gregory burrowed deep into the chest that held his belongings. From the very bottom he drew out a bundle of parchment sheets.

"Here," he said, "is the first illumination I ever did."

Smudge looked at the clumsy drawing. The faces on the saints were crooked, the eyes were crossed, the mouths looked like sausages.

In spite of his nervousness, Smudge had to laugh. "Oh, Brother Gregory, why are you making fun of me? Of course, that isn't your work. You are the finest illuminator of manuscripts in Ireland."

"It is my work. And so is this, and this, and this."

Brother Gregory showed Smudge sheet after sheet of faces twisted into ugly shapes, angel wings like the wings on a bat, beards and hair like tangled strands of straw, a lion that resembled a mouse. And worst of all—there were smudges!

"You mean I must do the same thing over and over?"

"Yes, until it is right."

"But it will never be right."

"Of course, it will. See here."

Brother Gregory turned to the last page of his book of mistakes. The paintings were as fine as the masterful work he did now.

"It will only take practice," he told Smudge. When he saw Smudge wince he said, "God gives us talent but we have to meet God halfway."

There were weeks of **a**'s. Thousands of **a**'s marched through Smudge's dreams. There was ink on his robe and ink on his hood and ink on his nose.

The snows fell silent as feathers on the monastery roof. The gulls flew south. The snows melted, the gulls returned to the island. The first bit of spring green poked up amongst the rocks. The monks had their yearly baths in preparation for Easter.

Smudge was working on his **e**'s. It was so hard to get that little enclosed space just the same in all the **e**'s without actually getting out a ruler and measuring but Brother Gregory wouldn't allow that.

"You must develop your eye," he said.

Brother Ethbert peeked into Brother Gregory's cell to see how the Christmas Story was coming along.

"He's only at the **e**'s," Brother Ethbert told Brother Bede.

Brother Bede gathered his courage and went to the abbot.

"Dear Abbot," he said, "it will be years before the Christmas Story is finished. Heaven forbid, but what if you never live to see it? Let Brother Ethbert do the lettering."

What Brother Bede could not know is that an angel had come to the abbot. At least the abbot thought it was an angel. It was something between a great shadow from the pine tree outside his window and a kind of rosy glow that comes over everything when the sun sinks down at the end of the day.

Because he was a little hard of hearing and because angels tend to whisper in your ear, what the abbot thought the angel said was that he would live to see the Christmas Story finished. The abbot knew the longer it took, the longer he would live.

"Don't bother me with details," the abbot told Brother Bede and sent him on his way.

The little green lettuces sprung up from the warm earth. There were cockles and winkles in the rock pools. There were fresh peas in the soup and strawberries for dessert. The feast days came and went.

At last Smudge drew a perfect **z**. The top looked firmly in one direction while the bottom explored an entirely different direction. A firm and decisive line drew them together.

"Let us begin," Brother Gregory said.

He took out his finest parchment. He set out his pots of paint: red ochre from the earth, the yellow of malachite, the brown of lichen, the green of verdigris, and the precious blue of lapis lazuli. In a secret formula known only to Brother Gregory the colors were mixed with white of egg, fish oil, and a smidgen of glue.

"You may rule the lines," he told Smudge.

Smudge had practiced lines until everything he saw was divided into horizontal sections. The lines he drew were perfect.

Brother Gregory marked the places where his illustrations would go, which initials he would embellish, and where along the margins his flourishes would decorate the text. He indicated the pages on which he would paint miniature scenes to illustrate the Christmas Story.

Smudge's hand trembled as he picked up his goose quill and dipped it in ink made of soot from slowly burning oak fires. Such ink would never fade. Smudge trembled, knowing that what he wrote would be there forever.

"*And it came to pass*," Smudge wrote.

The **A** stood on its own feet, legs apart, just daring you to defy it. The **n** had a gently curved top and just the slightest indication of looking to the right. The **d** put a firm end to the word.

When the first sentence was completed, Smudge turned to Brother Gregory, terrified lest Brother Gregory find fault. Brother Gregory gave an ear-to-ear grin.

"Smudge, that sentence is not only perfectly formed, but it is unique! You have made a sentence with letters in a manner no one else has ever attempted."

And it came to pass

Brother Gregory took up his brushes. As he worked, he groaned, he sighed, his forehead was pleated with wrinkles.

Frightened, Smudge asked, "Is there something wrong, Brother Gregory?"

"It is a pleasure to do one's best, Smudge, but there is also pain in the effort, for you always wish your work better than it is. Do you not find that is so?"

Smudge did. Wanting to make each letter perfect was a great strain, but when the well-formed letter stood there in all its black glory the pleasure was worth the pain.

There was no telling where Brother Gregory would find subjects for his drawings. When he was painting the scene of the stable where the Christ child lay, he studied the monastery's farm animals, the chickens and sheep and the monastery donkey. Even the monastery cats and the mice they chased found their way into his paintings.

One day a fly flew into the cell and Brother Gregory put it into a border he was painting.

"The image of a fly in a sacred illumination?" Smudge was shocked.

"Ah, Smudge," Brother Gregory said, "everything around us speaks of God's glory and the ordinary and simple things most of all."

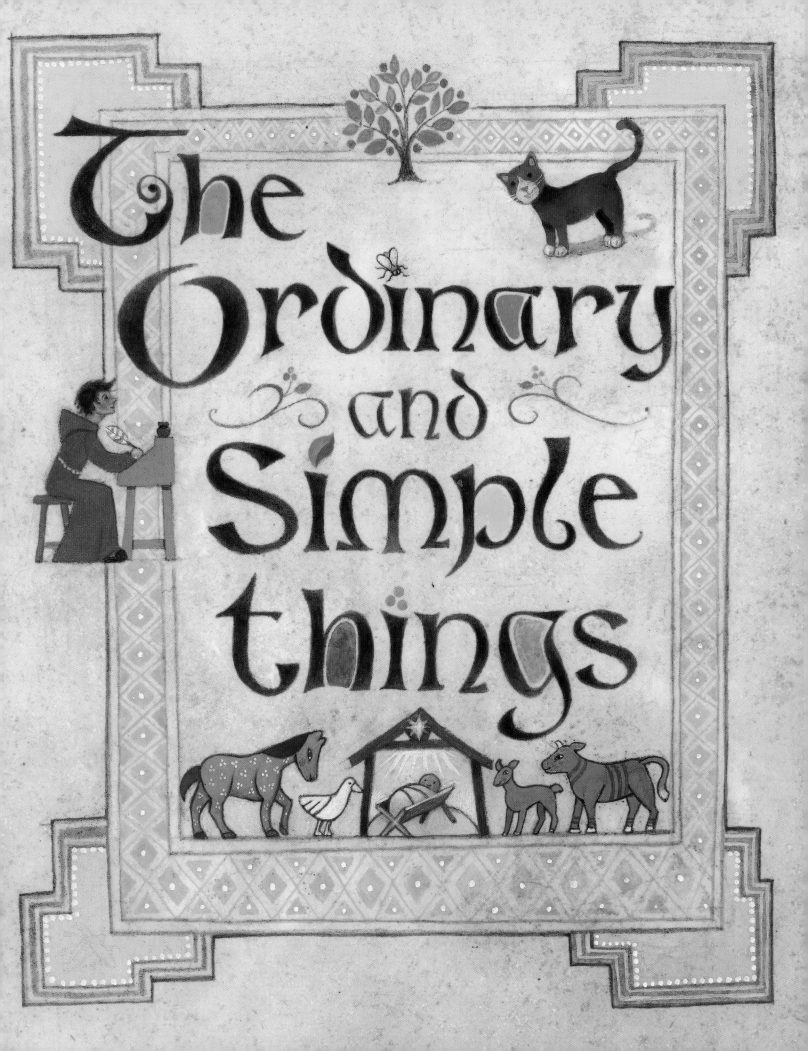

The Ordinary and Simple things

It was on the Feast of Saint Ita that Smudge made a mistake.

To celebrate the feast day the monks had honey with their bread. Eager to return to work Smudge did not take time to wash his hands. He picked up his goose quill and began to form a new paragraph beginning with the letter **B**. It was one of his favorites, for he loved its bumpiness.

The quill clung to his sticky fingers and the bumps in the **B** were two different sizes. The top bump was big and generous and the bottom bump was puny and stingy.

"Oh, Brother Gregory!" Smudge wailed. "Just look at the mistake I have made! I have ruined your beautiful sheet of parchment."

Brother Gregory frowned. He was as silent as the moment before a storm when the winds take a great gulp and get ready to blow. Smudge trembled.

Brother Gregory took up his brush. In the top bump he painted a flower in full bloom. In the bottom bump a delicate leaf.

"Always try to make an opportunity of your mistake, Smudge, and not a regret."

On Christmas morning the abbot and the monks gathered in the chapel. There was a special feast in honor of the day: apples for everyone, whortleberry jam on thick slabs of bread, cider to drink instead of water. Brother Gregory stood before the abbot, the manuscript of the finished Christmas Story in his hands.

The ancient and stubborn abbot was relieved to find that though the story was finished, he, himself, was very much alive. Could angels make a mistake? Probably not, but surely they could change their minds.

He looked at the familiar words put before him. The first letter of each paragraph had a small and perfect picture of the story the paragraph told. All the other letters were shapely and flawless. In a sinful show of pride he told himself no other monastery could boast a manuscript as fine as this one.

The abbot marveled at how a handful of letters could be placed first one way and then another to form words and the words used to make thoughts. Without words, thoughts would disappear and the whole world would have to begin each day with no lesson learned. Without letters there would be no knowledge of the Christmas promise made and the Christmas promise kept.

Smudge (now known as Brother Cuthbert) became the monastery's official scribe but he still looked the same. His robe still trailed on the floor, his sleeves covered his hands, his hood fell over his face. And like the rest of us, all his life he made mistakes.

To Maeve and Grady Nolan

Gloria

For Tai Melendy

Stephen

Sleeping Bear Press®
315 E. Eisenhower Parkway, Suite 200
Ann Arbor, MI 48108
www.sleepingbearpress.com

Sleeping Bear Press, a part of Cengage Learning.

10 9 8 7 6 5 4 3 2 1

Library of Congress Cataloging-in-Publication Data

Whelan, Gloria.
Smudge and the book of mistakes : a Christmas story / written by Gloria
Whelan ; illustrated by Stephen Costanza.
p. cm.
Summary: In Ireland in the Middle Ages, young Brother Cuthbert, known
for making mistakes and giving up easily, is chosen through a miscommunication
to serve as scribe for an illuminated manuscript of the Nativity story, through
which the Abbot hopes to make the monastery famous.
ISBN 978-1-58536-483-1 (hardback)
[1. Scribes--Fiction. 2. Monks--Fiction. 3. Monasteries--Fiction. 4.
Determination (Personality trait)--Fiction. 5. Middle Ages--Fiction. 6. Ireland--
History--To 1172--Fiction.] I. Costanza, Stephen, ill. II. Title.
PZ7.W5718Sn 2012
[Fic]--dc23   2012007576

Printed by China Translation & Printing Services Limited,
Guangdong Province, China. 1st printing. 06/2012